ZARA MENDONCA

Whispers in the Mezquita

Contents

1

Chapter 1

The sun was already high in the sky when Laila began her first tour of the day, casting a soft amber hue upon the grand pillars of the Mezquita. The ornate archways reflected the interplay of light and shadow, a visual testament to the architectural genius of the monument.

Gathering her group at the entrance, Laila greeted them with a warm smile. "Welcome, dear travelers, to the Great Mosque of Cordoba. Today, you'll not only walk through its corridors but travel back in time with its stories."

As they ventured further inside, the temperature dropped, and the coolness of the stone provided a welcome respite from the mid-morning heat. The group, a mix of curious scholars and enthusiastic tourists, huddled closer, hanging on Laila's every word.

"Built over 300 years ago, the Mezquita isn't just a place of worship but a symbol of Cordoba's cultural and religious harmony," Laila began, her voice echoing softly. "Its foundation lies on what was once a Visigothic church, a blend of both Moorish and Christian architectural techniques."

She led them to the majestic mihrab, the semicircular niche indicating the direction of Mecca. Its intricate mosaics shimmered, depicting geometric patterns and Arabic calligraphy.

"Do you hear the whisper of the walls?" Laila asked, a playful glint in her eyes. "Each brick here tells a tale. Of caliphs and commoners, of celebrations and conquests."

A young boy in the group raised his hand, "Did they hide treasures here?"

Laila chuckled, "Ah, tales of treasures. While we've no gold or jewels hidden away, the real treasure of the Mezquita lies in its history, its art, and the secrets it has witnessed over the centuries."

She continued her journey with the group, pointing out the various expansions the Mezquita underwent, and how the horseshoe arches were influenced by earlier Roman architecture.

As they approached the courtyard, the scent of orange blossoms greeted them. "This," Laila motioned grandly, "is the Patio de los Naranjos. A place of reflection, prayer, and often, many a clandestine rendezvous."

An elderly man from the group remarked, "You make history come alive, young lady. It feels like these walls indeed have secrets."

Laila winked, "And perhaps, dear sir, if the walls could talk, they might just share some with us."

Little did she know how soon that might come to pass.

***

As the tour wound down and the visitors dispersed, Laila took a moment to herself, perched on a stone bench in the Patio de los Naranjos. The gentle rustling of leaves and the occasional bird's chirp provided a peaceful backdrop. She loved these brief moments of tranquility amidst her hectic day, allowing her to reflect and recharge.

Before she could drift too deep into her thoughts, a hurried rustle of fabric caught her attention. Turning her gaze, she found her cousin Yasmine rushing towards her, her colorful skirts billowing around her.

"Laila," Yasmine gasped, slightly out of breath, "I've been searching all over for you."

Laila rose, concern etching her features. "What's the matter, Yasmine? You look flustered."

With a hesitant glance around, as if fearing eavesdroppers, Yasmine drew a folded parchment from her bag. The seal was already broken. "I received this mysterious letter this morning. It bears no name, but it speaks of the Mezquita and hints at secrets long buried."

Laila's eyebrows knitted in confusion. "A prank, perhaps?"

Yasmine shook her head, her long curls dancing with the motion. "That's what I thought too. But look." She unfolded the parchment, revealing an intricate drawing of the Mezquita from an aerial view. Various sections of the mosque were marked with symbols Laila couldn't immediately decipher.

Laila traced the drawing with her fingers, intrigue bubbling within her. "This is detailed. Too detailed for a mere prank."

Yasmine whispered, "There's a note." She pointed at the bottom, where a message was inscribed in a delicate script:

"To the keeper of the Mezquita's tales,
In shadows of history, truth prevails.
Seek the heart where two worlds blend,
And you'll unearth secrets that time did mend."

Laila's eyes gleamed with excitement. "A riddle! But why send it to you?"

Yasmine shrugged, her anxiety evident. "I'm just a seller of fabrics. This has nothing to do with me. But you... you know the Mezquita like the back of your hand."

Laila mulled over the message, her natural curiosity piqued. "It might be nothing, but it could be a fascinating mystery. Let's see where this leads."

As the two women pondered over the enigmatic letter, the golden hues of the setting sun bathed the Mezquita, casting longer shadows and promising secrets yet to be unveiled.

***

The hustle and bustle of the evening prayers began to fill the Mezquita. The familiar, comforting sounds of recitations and the soft hum of chatter created a serene atmosphere. Laila and Yasmine, still engrossed in the mysterious letter, found a secluded corner away from the prayer-goers to discuss their next steps.

Suddenly, a soft, raspy voice interrupted their conversation. "Playing with riddles, are we?"

The two women turned to find Farida, the elderly historian. Her once-vibrant eyes, now clouded with age, always held a certain depth to them—a well of knowledge and wisdom. Draped in a deep blue shawl, she used her walking stick more for emphasis than support.

"Farida," Laila greeted with a smile, holding up the letter, "You always seem to appear at the most curious moments."

Farida's gaze locked onto the parchment, her eyes narrowing slightly. "I've seen similar before. Years ago. Such things are not to be taken lightly."

Yasmine's unease grew. "Is it... dangerous?"

Laila, ever the skeptic, interjected, "It's just a drawing and a poem, Farida. What harm could it possibly bring?"

Farida, however, looked gravely at the two women. "It's not the letter you should be wary of, but the happenings it might herald. Lately, I've felt a shift in the Mezquita. The shadows grow longer, the nights quieter. The very walls seem to whisper."

Laila raised an eyebrow, intrigued. "What kind of whispers?"

Farida leaned in closer. "Cries from the past, perhaps. Old memories, long-buried truths, yearning to resurface. Every night, I hear soft footsteps where there should be none, fleeting glimpses of figures that disappear before I can truly see them."

Laila felt a chill run down her spine, her skepticism momentarily shaken. "Ghosts?"

The elderly historian shrugged. "Or memories. The Mezquita has stood witness to centuries of history, my dear. It holds more secrets than any of us can fathom."

Laila frowned, torn between her innate curiosity and the unsettling warning. "So, what do you suggest we do?"

Farida sighed, her gaze distant. "Tread carefully. Seek the truth, by all means, but remember that some things are buried for a reason."

With that ominous advice, Farida continued on her way, leaving Laila and Yasmine with more questions than answers. The weight of the Mezquita's history pressed upon them, hinting at the mysteries they were about to unravel.

2

Chapter 2

Laila had barely slept, the mysterious letter and Farida's warnings weighing heavily on her mind. By dawn, she found herself back at the Mezquita, seeking answers. She needed a perspective grounded in the physical realm and knew just the person to approach: Ismail, the lead architect overseeing the ongoing restoration of the mosque.

As she approached the eastern wing, she found Ismail surrounded by scrolls and sketches, intently discussing something with his team. The air was thick with dust, the scent of aged wood and stone hinting at the many layers of history they were unearthing.

"Ismail!" Laila called out, her voice echoing slightly.

The tall, bearded man looked up, his face breaking into a broad smile upon seeing her. "Laila! To what do I owe this early visit?"

Laila wasted no time, producing the mysterious letter and drawing. "Have you seen anything like this in your findings?"

Ismail took the parchment, his brow furrowing as he studied it. "Interesting... This is an unusually detailed sketch, and these symbols..." He traced the symbols lightly with his fingers.

"They're not unfamiliar."

A spark of hope ignited in Laila's eyes. "You've seen them before?"

"Indeed," Ismail nodded, "While we've been restoring, we've come across some hidden compartments and inscriptions. These symbols seem to correlate with markings we've discovered in the older sections of the Mezquita."

Laila's heart raced. "Could they point to something specific? Something hidden?"

Ismail paused, considering her question. "It's possible. Many places of worship have secrets, either to protect valuable items or knowledge. Given the age and history of the Mezquita, it wouldn't surprise me."

Laila, ever eager, pressed on. "Can I see these markings?"

Ismail chuckled, "Always the curious one, aren't you? Come."

He led Laila through a labyrinth of scaffolding, stopping at a semi-restored archway. There, carved into the stone, were symbols strikingly similar to those on the letter.

"These," Ismail pointed, "were covered by plasterwork from a later period. We believe it might've been a way to protect or conceal whatever these symbols represented."

Laila traced the carvings, the texture rough against her fingertips. The mystery was becoming tangible, and she was more determined than ever to uncover it.

"Promise me caution, Laila," Ismail's voice broke her reverie. "Unraveling the past is a delicate task. One must be prepared for what they might find."

Laila nodded, her resolve unwavering. "Thank you, Ismail. This is just the beginning."

As they retreated from the depths of the Mezquita, the morning sun illuminated the mosque, casting a golden hue over the old stones and hinting at the secrets they harbored.

***

Guided by the symbols, Laila and Ismail found themselves in one of the less frequented sections of the Mezquita. The air was cooler here, thick with the scent of moss and forgotten centuries. The walls were beautifully adorned, yet worn, holding onto their secrets with resilience.

"There's something odd about this wall," Laila mused, studying the patterns. The intricate designs seemed to dance around a particular point, drawing the observer's attention towards the center.

Ismail, bringing his expertise into play, ran his fingers over the surface. "It seems... hollow," he remarked, tapping lightly to illustrate. The sound confirmed his suspicion. Behind the solid façade, there was a void.

Summoning a couple of his workmen, Ismail instructed them to carefully chisel away at the marked section. Each strike of the chisel was met with bated breath, the weight of history evident in the room.

Slowly, as the outer layer gave way, an ornate wooden door with brass detailing was revealed, its surface marked by the same symbols as the letter. Laila's eyes widened in astonishment. "A hidden chamber, here, in the Mezquita?"

Ismail, equally intrigued, gently pushed on the door. It resisted at first, but with a soft creak, it reluctantly yielded, revealing a dimly lit room beyond.

The chamber, bathed in an eerie glow from a small oculus above, was surprisingly intact. The walls were lined with bookshelves, each holding scrolls and manuscripts. In the center stood a wooden table, its surface covered in dust and more scrolls. Artifacts, possibly of religious or cultural significance, were meticulously placed in various corners.

"It's a library," Laila whispered, reverence in her voice. "Or perhaps a study?"

Ismail nodded, equally awed. "A repository of knowledge, hidden away. But why?"

Laila approached the table, her fingers gingerly picking up a scroll. Unfurling it, she discovered detailed architectural plans of the Mezquita, annotated in a script she didn't immediately recognize.

As she scanned the room, a particular manuscript caught her eye. It was bound in leather, embossed with gold, and placed prominently on a pedestal, as if of great importance. As she approached, she realized the symbols on its cover mirrored those on the mysterious letter.

"This," she murmured, holding up the manuscript, "might just be the key to our riddle."

The chamber, silent for possibly centuries, was now alive with possibilities. Every item, every manuscript, held a tale, and Laila was determined to hear them all.

***

The air grew stiller as Laila and Ismail continued their exploration of the concealed chamber. With every scroll they unfurled and every artifact they examined, the weight of the past pressed more heavily upon them. But nothing could have prepared them for what lay in the chamber's shadowy corner.

As Laila shifted a heavy curtain, her eyes widened in horror. There, concealed from initial view, lay an ancient skeleton, its bones resting as if in eternal contemplation. Beside it was a small, worn-out leather bag and a collection of papers.

Ismail rushed over, the color draining from his face. "This... this is no ordinary burial."

Laila nodded, swallowing hard. "No grave goods, no ceremonial positioning. It looks... abrupt."

Drawing closer, Laila's attention was caught by a glimmer at the skeleton's chest. A stunning amulet, shaped like the crescent moon and adorned with deep blue lapis lazuli, lay nestled against the age-old bones. It looked out of place, its sheen still vibrant, untouched by the passage of time.

Gently lifting it, Laila marveled at its craftsmanship. "This isn't just decorative. It's symbolic, possibly ceremonial."

Ismail, ever the practical one, motioned to the papers. "These might provide answers." He gingerly picked up the topmost sheet, his eyes scanning the ancient script. "It's a mix of Arabic and an older, local dialect."

Laila took a moment to study the amulet further. A series of inscriptions ran along its edges, the script matching the mysterious symbols from the letter and the room's door. "Ismail, these symbols... they're here too."

Ismail, deep in the manuscript, nodded absently. "This speaks of a guardian, a protector of the Mezquita's deepest secrets. Someone who took an oath to shield its mysteries, even unto death."

A shiver ran down Laila's spine. "Could this be...?"

"The guardian?" Ismail finished, looking solemnly at the skeletal remains. "It's very possible."

Laila clutched the amulet, feeling an odd warmth emanating from it. "Then this," she whispered, "is a key. A key to a mystery that's been buried for centuries."

The two stood in the chamber, the weight of their discovery settling upon them. They had unearthed more than just a hidden room; they had stumbled upon a tale of devotion, sacrifice, and unsolved enigmas. The journey to decode the Mezquita's mysteries had only just begun.

3

Chapter 3

Word travels fast, especially in a city as vibrant and closely-knit as Cordoba. By the time the first call to prayer echoed through the streets, murmurs about the discovery in the Mezquita had already begun to spread.

Laila, enjoying a quiet breakfast in the city's bustling marketplace, couldn't help but overhear snippets of conversations from neighboring tables.

"Did you hear? They found a room in the Mezquita, sealed for centuries!"

"They say there's a skeleton, a guardian of some sort."

"And that amulet... I heard it's cursed! Whoever holds it is doomed."

Laila's fingers instinctively clutched the pendant she wore beneath her robes, the very same amulet they had discovered. She had felt a strange connection to it, deciding to wear it in hopes of understanding its mysteries better.

A voice interrupted her thoughts. "Laila! Is it true? The stories about the chamber?"

She looked up to find Rashid, a local merchant known for his love of gossip. His eyes were wide with excitement and curiosity.

Laila sighed, "Rashid, you know better than to believe every rumor you hear."

He leaned in, lowering his voice. "But there is some truth, isn't there? The whispers about the cursed chamber?"

Laila took a deep breath, choosing her words carefully. "We found a room, yes, with historical artifacts and manuscripts. As for curses, I believe they're often born from fear of the unknown."

Rashid seemed slightly disappointed but nodded thoughtfully. "Still, discoveries like this... they change things, Laila. The city will be buzzing for weeks."

Laila smiled wryly, "Let them buzz. It's the truth that matters, not tales spun by idle minds."

However, as the day wore on, Laila couldn't shake off an unsettling feeling. The rumors, though exaggerated, held a grain of truth. And with truth came responsibility. The Mezquita's secrets were unraveling, and she found herself at the very heart of the mystery.

***

The sun had reached its zenith when Commander Rashid al-Mansur, distinct from Rashid the merchant, entered the Mezquita's vast courtyard. Cordoba, under the Almohad dynasty, was a center of power, culture, and diversity. Christians, Jews, and Muslims coexisted in an era of relative harmony, but political shifts were always afoot. The Almohads, who had taken over from the fractured Taifas, sought to establish a unified rule over Andalucía. Yet, tensions ran high as neighboring taifas, once independent principalities, often threatened the city's stability.

His imposing figure, adorned in polished armor and followed by a retinue of guards, drew the attention of many. His role as the city's chief military and security officer made his involvement all the more significant in these volatile times.

Laila and Ismail, deeply engrossed in discussing the political intricacies and the possible ramifications of their find, noticed his entrance. They exchanged glances, a mix of anticipation and concern.

Commander al-Mansur beckoned them, his stern face echoing the seriousness of the era. "Laila. Ismail. Word of your discovery has reached even the Emir's court, especially in these times when our dynasty is ensuring the coexistence of all faiths. I am here to ensure the security of our city's heritage."

Ismail, acknowledging the political atmosphere, bowed respectfully. "Commander, amidst the changing dynamics of Andalucía and the ever-present threats from former taifas, we too share that concern. Our discovery was unexpected, and we're still trying to fathom its political and historical implications."

Al-Mansur's eyes, reflecting the wisdom of navigating the political maze of Andalucía, scanned the surroundings. "I will need a full account of your findings. In these times, any artifact, any document, could hold strategic significance."

Laila, aware of the rich tapestry of faiths and politics, stepped forward. "Commander, we aim to shed light on the Mezquita's history, a history where diverse faiths thrived side by side."

The commander's gaze met hers. "History often intertwines with the present, Laila. While your pursuit is commendable, it may also unearth sensitive truths, truths that may ripple through our already intricate political landscape."

The trio, followed by guards aware of the city's delicate balance, made their way to the chamber. The atmosphere grew dense as Commander al-Mansur processed the scene before him.

Laila hesitated before revealing, "The amulet... I've safeguarded it, feeling its connection to a time when Cordoba was a beacon of harmony."

Al-Mansur, acknowledging the weight of her statement, responded, "Every piece of this puzzle must be accounted for. Bring it to me by tomorrow. Its significance may be more profound than we imagine."

As the commander and his entourage departed, Laila and Ismail, with the backdrop of Cordoba's complex history, were left contemplating the intertwining threads of past and present.

***

As evening cast its golden hues upon the city, Laila found herself in the abode of Naima, an elderly scholar known for her vast knowledge of Andalusian history and a rumored intimate connection with the early founders of the Kabbalah. Surrounding her were walls lined with scrolls, tablets, and ancient texts that had witnessed the passage of time. Some, if one looked closely, bore symbols reminiscent of Jewish mysticism.

Laila carefully unveiled the amulet, placing it on a cloth in front of the wise woman. Naima's eyes, although clouded with age, sparkled with a hint of recognition as they settled upon the piece.

"It's exquisite," Naima whispered, her fingers lightly tracing the inscriptions. "And familiar. The symbols, they hold traces of ancient Kabbalistic knowledge."

Laila leaned forward, intrigued. "You recognize it?"

Naima nodded slowly. "Not this exact piece, but its design and symbols. This amulet represents the moon, a symbol of guidance, reflection, and protection, often revered in our mystic traditions."

Laila's thoughts drifted to the skeleton, the so-called guardian. "Could it have belonged to someone of importance?"

Naima, her eyes distant, began recounting a tale. "Centuries ago, during the early days of the Mezquita, a lineage of guardians was established. These individuals, chosen for their integrity, wisdom, and perhaps a deep spiritual connection, were tasked with safeguarding the mosque's secrets and treasures. They bore a symbol of their station—an amulet."

Laila's heart raced. "This amulet?"

Naima nodded. "If it's genuine, then yes. It would mean that the guardian you found was one of the last, if not the last, of that lineage."

A heavy silence filled the room. The weight of history, of duty and sacrifice, pressed upon Laila's shoulders. The amulet wasn't just a relic; it was a testament to an age-old oath intertwined with threads of mysticism.

"The symbols," Laila began, pointing to the inscriptions, "they appear elsewhere in the Mezquita. Can they be deciphered?"

Drawing from her depth of knowledge, Naima hesitated, then began translating. "They speak of light in darkness, of truth revealed to those who seek. Infused with Kabbalistic overtones, they're both a promise and a warning."

Laila clutched the amulet, its significance now even more profound. "I must return it to its rightful place, ensure its safety."

Naima's gaze met hers, filled with a mix of wisdom and caution. "In uncovering the past, Laila, remember that some secrets, especially those with roots in mysticism, are protected for a reason."

Laila left Naima's abode with a sense of purpose. The amulet was more than just an artifact; it was a beacon that connected past and present, beckoning her deeper into the heart of the mystery.

4

Chapter 4

Laila's journey took her next to the outskirts of Cordoba, where Farida, the city's renowned seer, resided. Unlike Naima's abode, filled with manuscripts and the tangible weight of history, Farida's dwelling was filled with the ethereal - dream catchers, vials of scents, and candles of all shapes and colors.

Farida, a woman draped in layers of flowing fabric with eyes that seemed to pierce the very soul, welcomed Laila with a knowing smile. "You come bearing the weight of ages," she observed.

Laila, unfolding the cloth to reveal the amulet, replied, "I seek to understand its essence, its energy."

Farida leaned forward, her fingers hovering over the amulet without touching it. Her eyes closed, and her breathing deepened. A quiet fell over the room, broken only by the faint whisper of the wind outside.

After what felt like an eternity, Farida opened her eyes. "This amulet... It's a nexus of energies. A binding force between two realms."

Laila, captivated, asked, "What realms?"

"The seen and the unseen. The world we know and the one that exists in shadows," Farida replied, her voice taking on a haunting quality. "The guardian who bore this amulet walked between these realms, serving as a bridge."

Laila pondered on this revelation. "And the inscriptions?"

"They're a code," Farida revealed. "Not just of words, but of intent, of emotions. They bind the amulet's bearer to the Mezquita, ensuring its protection across time."

Laila thought of the skeleton, the guardian who had seemingly given his life in service. "Is there a way to unlock this code? To communicate with this guardian's spirit?"

Farida hesitated. "It's possible, but not without risks. The amulet is a conduit. Using it to reach out could draw energies, not all of which are benevolent."

Laila, determination evident in her gaze, responded, "I must know. The Mezquita's secrets are intertwined with this amulet, and I need to understand them."

Farida, recognizing Laila's resolve, nodded slowly. "Very well. But tread with caution. The path you're about to embark upon is filled with shadows, and not all may be dispelled by light."

As Laila departed, the weight of Farida's words settled upon her. She was not just unearthing history; she was delving into realms unknown, and the journey promised to be as perilous as it was enlightening.

***

The Cordoba market was a hive of activity. Stalls lined the narrow streets, their wares displayed in vibrant arrays. The scents of spices, fresh bread, and simmering stews filled the air. But amidst the usual hustle and bustle, a different kind of energy pulsed – one of intrigue and speculation.

As Laila navigated through the maze of vendors, she caught hushed conversations that piqued her interest.

"I heard Kareem is offering a hefty sum for any information about the chamber," murmured a spice merchant to his neighbor.

The other replied, "Of course he is. Kareem always has his fingers in every hidden pot of gold. But this isn't gold, it's history!"

Laila's ears perked up at the mention of Kareem. A wealthy trader with rumored ties to underground networks, Kareem had an infamous reputation for seeking out rare and valuable artifacts. His interests were seldom academic; he was driven by profit.

She approached a jewelry vendor, pretending to admire a bracelet. "Have you heard anything about Kareem and the Mezquita discovery?"

The vendor, an old woman with a keen eye for gossip, leaned in conspiratorially. "Word is he's desperate to get his hands on the amulet. Thinks it'll fetch a fortune in distant lands."

Laila, feigning nonchalance, pressed on. "Why? It's just a relic."

The woman chuckled. "For you and me, perhaps. But for those who know its true value... well, let's just say there are many who'd kill to possess it."

A chill ran down Laila's spine. The stakes were higher than she'd realized. The amulet wasn't just a key to history; it was a magnet for power and greed.

As Laila left the market, her thoughts raced. She needed to safeguard the amulet, not just from the potential dangers it posed, but from those who sought to exploit it. With Kareem's intentions now clear, the mystery had taken on a new, more sinister dimension.

***

After her enlightening visit to the market, Laila decided to once again seek the counsel of Naima. With the weight of the amulet around her neck, she stepped into the familiar embrace of Naima's abode, the gentle scent of old parchment comforting her.

Naima looked up, sensing Laila's heightened urgency. "Back so soon? What weighs on your mind, child?"

Laila relayed her encounter at the market, detailing Kareem's apparent interest in the amulet. As she spoke, she saw Naima's eyes darken with concern.

After a reflective pause, Naima said, "The allure of power, of possessing something unique, can drive even the wisest to folly."

Laila sighed. "I need to understand this amulet, to unlock its mysteries before it falls into the wrong hands."

Naima nodded thoughtfully. "Perhaps there is a way. In my readings, I've come across mentions of an elixir, an ancient potion said to grant clarity of vision to those seeking truths hidden in the arcane."

Laila's heart raced. "An elixir connected to the amulet?"

Naima fetched a weathered scroll, its edges frayed with time. "According to this," she began, tracing the script with her finger, "the guardians of the Mezquita used this potion to enhance their connection to the amulet, revealing visions and insights. It was named the 'Elixir of Revelation.'"

Laila leaned in, captivated. "Could we recreate it?"

Naima hesitated. "The ingredients are rare, and the preparation is meticulous. Additionally, the elixir is potent; its effects can be unpredictable."

Laila, her determination unwavering, responded, "It's a risk I'm willing to take. If it provides clarity, sheds light on the amulet's purpose, then it's a path I must explore."

Naima, recognizing Laila's resolve, agreed. "Very well. We shall prepare the elixir. But remember, revelations can be both enlightening and overwhelming. Tread carefully, Laila."

As they began their preparations, Laila felt a mixture of excitement and apprehension. The amulet's enigma was deepening, and the elixir promised to be a catalyst in unveiling its secrets.

5

Chapter 5

The next morning, Laila found herself at the Mezquita once more, drawn by the allure of its secrets. She met with Ismail, who had been closely studying the artifacts and remnants found within the hidden chamber.

The morning sun streamed through the mosque's windows, casting a soft glow on the intricate mosaics and arches. Laila, her thoughts heavy with the recent revelations, greeted Ismail. "Any new findings?"

Ismail, his face a canvas of excitement and reverence, nodded. "We've made an interesting discovery about the guardian, the skeleton in the chamber." He carefully spread out a parchment which bore the image of a sigil - a crescent moon enveloped by the outline of a hand.

Laila's gaze settled on the emblem. "It looks similar to the amulet."

Ismail nodded. "Indeed. We cross-referenced this sigil with historical records. It appears to be the personal emblem of a priest named Yunus who vanished without a trace some two centuries ago. He was revered, known for his wisdom, piety, and his role as a mediator between the realms of the living and the unseen."

Laila, connecting the dots, murmured, "A bridge… like Farida mentioned."

Ismail continued, "Yunus was rumored to have knowledge of sacred rituals, protective spells, and ancient lore that few possessed. His sudden disappearance was a great mystery. Many believed he had ascended, while others whispered that he had been taken by the unseen forces he communed with."

Laila pondered on this. "Could the guardian in the chamber be Yunus?"

"It's a distinct possibility," Ismail replied, his voice filled with awe. "If it's true, the chamber could have been his final resting place, a sanctum where he continued his guardianship from beyond the veil."

The implications were profound. The guardian, potentially Yunus, had dedicated his existence, both in life and death, to the Mezquita and its secrets. The amulet wasn't just a relic; it was a bridge between worlds, a testament to undying devotion.

Laila felt a surge of responsibility. "We must honor him, ensure his legacy remains protected."

Ismail nodded in agreement. "His story, his dedication… it deserves to be known and revered."

As they left the chamber, Laila felt an even deeper connection to the Mezquita's past. The discovery of the potential identity of the guardian added yet another layer to the unfolding tapestry of mystery.

***

Laila had barely stepped outside the Mezquita's walls when she ran into Ahmed, a local storyteller known for his vast knowledge of folklore and Cordoba's history. His presence at the Mezquita wasn't unusual, as he often regaled visitors with tales of the past.

Seeing her deep in thought, Ahmed greeted her with a warm smile. "Laila! Lost in the annals of time?"

She returned his smile, grateful for the distraction. "Ahmed, always with a tale on the tip of your tongue. Do you know any stories connected to a priest named Yunus?"

Ahmed's eyes gleamed with recognition. "Ah, Yunus... The priest who whispered to the moon. Sit, sit!" He gestured to a nearby bench, and they both settled down.

He began, "Long ago, when the Mezquita's stones still gleamed with the sheen of newness, Yunus served as its beacon of light. His prayers were said to have a power, a purity, that few could match."

Laila listened intently as Ahmed painted a vivid picture of Yunus, kneeling under the Mezquita's dome, praying on a moonlit night.

"One evening, during a particularly radiant full moon, Yunus stood in the heart of the Mezquita, reciting verses that echoed with both lament and hope. The tale goes that as he prayed, the moon's light intensified, converging upon the amulet he wore. The very amulet you now seek answers about."

Laila's breath caught. The story was weaving a spell around her.

Ahmed continued, "The light from the moon and the amulet's glow merged, creating a luminous portal. From it emerged ethereal figures, guardians of old, who joined Yunus in his prayer. The Mezquita was bathed in a celestial glow, a beacon for all of Cordoba to witness."

Laila whispered, "What happened then?"

Ahmed sighed, "The portal lasted but a few moments, vanishing as the final notes of Yunus's prayer faded. But those who witnessed it spoke of an overwhelming sense of peace, of unity between realms. Yunus had, for a brief moment, bridged the gap between our world and the next."

He leaned closer, "It's said that the power of that prayer, that connection, was infused into the amulet. And Yunus, realizing the magnitude of what he held, dedicated his life to guarding it."

Laila was entranced, the weight of the amulet's history pressing upon her heart. "Thank you, Ahmed. Every piece of this story brings me closer to understanding the depth of its significance."

Ahmed nodded, "History is not just in the stones or relics, Laila, but in the stories we pass down. Remember, the past often speaks in whispers, and it's up to us to listen."

As she left Ahmed, the sun setting behind him, Laila felt even more anchored to her mission. The Mezquita wasn't just a historical monument; it was a vessel of stories, legends, and spirits that transcended time.

***

The streets of Cordoba grew busier as the day went on, with merchants calling out to potential buyers and the melodies of musicians filling the air. Laila, seeking some respite, decided to visit the city's renowned library, a treasure trove of ancient texts and scrolls.

As she entered the hallowed halls, the familiar face of Zaid, the chief librarian and an old friend of her family, greeted her. With a keen eye and an even keener mind, Zaid had aided her in many of her historical quests.

"Laila! It's been a while," Zaid exclaimed, his face lighting up. "What brings you to these parts?"

She smiled, "Seeking knowledge, as always. I'm looking for anything that might shed light on this." She showed him the amulet.

Zaid's eyes widened in recognition. "Ah, the guardian's amulet. I've seen something that might help." With that, he disappeared into one of the aisles, leaving Laila in a state of anticipation.

Moments later, he returned with a dusty old script, its pages yellowed with age. "This," he began, "is one of the lesser-known scripts detailing some of the Mezquita's hidden secrets."

Laila, eagerly taking the script, began to skim its contents. One section in particular caught her eye. It described a ritual involving the amulet, the moon, and a specific incantation.

Zaid, noticing her interest, added, "It's believed that this ritual allowed the guardian, presumably Yunus, to converse with the spirits of the Mezquita. But it comes with a warning. The ritual should only be performed with pure intent, lest it backfire."

Laila's heart raced. This script could potentially unlock the amulet's powers. "Zaid, this is invaluable. Thank you."

He smiled warmly. "The pursuit of knowledge is noble, Laila. Just remember, with great power comes great responsibility."

As she left the library, script in hand, Laila felt a mixture of excitement and trepidation. The path to understanding the amulet was becoming clearer, but with it came potential dangers she had to navigate with care.

6

Chapter 6

The courtyard of Hana's residence, draped in soft lantern light, was abuzz with Cordoba's elite and scholarly. Fragrances of blooming jasmine intertwined with the scent of sweet pastries. It was the much-awaited poetry evening, an event Hana hosted monthly to celebrate the arts.

Laila, taking a break from her quest, had decided to attend, hoping to immerse herself in the lyrical world of verse and melody. As she sipped on a cup of mint tea, Hana gracefully took the stage, her voice melodic and soothing as she began reciting her compositions.

However, as the night progressed, Rima, known for her sharp wit and even sharper tongue, requested a chance to share a few lines. She was known to be competitive, often seeking opportunities to outshine Hana.

With a sly smile, she began:

"In the heart of ancient stones, secrets lay,
  Guarded by spirits, night and day.
  Whispers of power, an amulet's gleam,

Unveil the truth or chase a dream."

The crowd murmured in appreciation, but Laila tensed, sensing the veiled hints directed towards the Mezquita mystery.

Rima continued, her eyes occasionally flitting towards Laila:

"Seeker of truths, tread with care,

For some paths lead to despair.

Guarded chambers, moonlit rites,

Beware the allure of forbidden sights."

The applause that followed was polite but filled with undertones of unease. Hana, ever the gracious host, thanked Rima for her verses. However, her eyes held a hint of concern.

Laila approached Rima, her curiosity piqued. "Those were intriguing lines, Rima. Inspired by recent events, perhaps?"

Rima smirked, playing coy. "Just the musings of an observant poet, dear Laila. Sometimes, inspiration is drawn from the world around us."

Laila nodded, not rising to the bait. "Indeed. And sometimes, mysteries are best left to those who understand their depths."

Rima's playful demeanor faltered for a moment, but she quickly recovered. "Just a friendly warning, Laila. Not all quests have happy endings."

As the evening wore on, Laila couldn't shake off the unease. Rima's words, though shrouded in poetic ambiguity, held a clear warning. The stakes of her quest were rising, and it was evident that more than just the walls of the Mezquita were watching.

***

As the poetry evening gradually morphed into smaller gatherings of discussion, Laila found herself wandering towards the gardens, seeking solace in its tranquility. The bubbling fountain and the muted glow from lanterns strewn across pathways offered a quiet contrast to the evening's charged atmosphere.

Lost in thought, Laila barely noticed Majid, the treasurer for the Mezquita's restoration fund, approach her. His usually jovial face looked strained and pensive.

"Laila," he began, glancing around to ensure their conversation would remain private. "I've been meaning to discuss something with you, especially given your close involvement with the Mezquita's history."

She turned to him, intrigued. "What is it, Majid?"

He hesitated, as if measuring his words. "Since the discovery of the chamber and the amulet, there's been a significant increase in donations for the Mezquita's restoration. At first, it seemed like a blessing. But recently, some of these generous donors have been... making demands."

Laila frowned. "Demands? What kind of demands?"

Majid looked visibly uncomfortable. "They wish to have exclusive access to certain areas of the Mezquita, specifically the newly discovered chamber. They also wish to be present during any further excavations."

Laila's alarm grew. "That's highly unusual. Do you know why they're so interested?"

Majid shook his head. "Not exactly. But whispers suggest they're part of an elite group with a keen interest in ancient relics, particularly those with rumored mystical properties."

She felt a chill run down her spine. "The amulet."

Majid nodded gravely. "I fear so. And while their financial support is beneficial, I'm worried about the strings attached. The Mezquita isn't just a historical site; it's a place of worship, reverence. We can't let it become a playground for the elite."

Laila agreed. "We need to tread carefully. The amulet and its mysteries are intertwined with the Mezquita's sanctity. We can't let outside influences dictate our approach."

Majid sighed in relief. "I'm glad you understand. I wasn't sure whom to turn to, but I knew you'd grasp the gravity of the situation."

Laila placed a reassuring hand on his arm. "We'll find a way to balance the restoration needs without compromising the Mezquita's integrity."

As Majid departed, Laila felt the weight of the task ahead. The layers of the mystery were becoming more intricate, now entangled with power plays and hidden agendas. She knew she'd have to be cautious and shrewd in her next moves.

***

Laila, still reeling from her conversation with Majid, was startled by a soft voice behind her. "You seem lost in thought."

She turned to find Nasir, an elderly man with a reputation for being the unofficial chronicler of Cordoba's streets. The deep creases on his face hinted at a lifetime of stories and experiences. He was the kind of man whose eyes sparkled with secrets of the past.

"Nasir," Laila greeted with warmth. "Always a pleasure."

He smiled, nodding. "I overheard snippets of your talk with Majid. The Mezquita's allure grows day by day, doesn't it?"

She hesitated before confiding, "It's not just the Mezquita, but what lies beneath."

Nasir's eyebrows rose, his interest piqued. "Ah, the underbelly of Cordoba. Did you know, dear Laila, that our city, especially around the Mezquita, is riddled with underground passages?"

Laila looked at him in surprise. "I knew of some, but not specifically linked to the Mezquita."

Nasir leaned in, his voice dropping to a whisper. "Old tales suggest these tunnels were once used by priests and guardians to move without being seen, especially during times of strife. Some even say these tunnels housed sacred relics, protecting them from invaders."

Laila's mind raced. If such tunnels existed, then the amulet and the skeleton might just be the tip of the iceberg. "Do you think one of these passages might lead to the newly discovered chamber?"

Nasir looked thoughtful. "It's possible. The chamber's location does align with some of the rumored tunnel routes. But these pathways haven't been used in centuries, and finding an entrance now would be a daunting task."

She pondered this new information. "Nasir, if there's a chance these tunnels hold more secrets related to the amulet, I need to explore them."

He smiled, a glint of mischief in his eyes. "Always the curious one. But remember, Laila, the underground can be deceptive. Take care not to lose yourself in its depths."

With that cryptic warning, Nasir bid her farewell, leaving Laila with a newfound determination to uncover the Mezquita's hidden labyrinth and the secrets it might conceal.

7

Chapter 7

As the sun cast its golden hues over Cordoba, Laila met Ismail at the outer perimeter of the Mezquita. Their mission for the day was clear: find an entrance to the fabled underground passages.

Ismail, with his intricate knowledge of the structure's architecture, was the perfect ally for such an expedition. He greeted Laila with an excited grin, "I've always heard tales of the Mezquita's underground world. Never thought I'd be searching for it."

Laila nodded, her determination evident. "We start by examining the foundation. The older sections of the Mezquita might give us a hint. Nasir's tales suggested that these entrances were hidden in plain sight."

Together, they began their meticulous exploration, poring over ancient stone floors, walls, and columns, occasionally consulting the blueprints Ismail had managed to procure.

Hours seemed to merge as one, with no immediate success. Just as frustration began to set in, Laila's keen eyes noticed an unusual pattern on the floor near a secluded alcove. An almost imperceptible outline of what seemed to be a trapdoor, covered in years of grime and dust, making it blend seamlessly with the surrounding tiles.

She called Ismail over, "Look here! This seems... out of place."

Ismail's eyes widened as he examined the pattern. Gently, using a small chisel, he began to work around the outline. As the seal broke, a hidden hatch creaked open, revealing a staircase leading into darkness.

A gust of cold, ancient air met them, carrying with it the scent of old parchment, dust, and an eerie silence that spoke of centuries of secrets.

Laila whispered, her voice echoing slightly, "The underground passages of the Mezquita. They're real."

Ismail, his excitement evident, replied, "This could be our gateway to understanding the amulet's mysteries."

Laila lit a lantern, its soft glow illuminating the first few steps. "We venture into the heart of history. Let's tread carefully."

And with that, the duo began their descent, the weight of centuries surrounding them as they delved deeper into the shadows of the past.

***

As Laila and Ismail ventured deeper into the tunnel, the ambient sounds of the Mezquita faded, replaced by a deep silence occasionally interrupted by the distant drip of water or the soft echo of their footsteps. The passage, illuminated by their lantern's flicker, revealed ornate carvings on its walls, long-forgotten inscriptions, and a sense of timelessness.

However, the deeper they went, the more intricate and maze-like the tunnels became. After what felt like hours, they stumbled upon a vast underground chamber filled with old manuscripts, artifacts, and faded murals depicting stories from a bygone era.

In their wonderment, they hardly noticed the soft click that echoed through the chamber. Turning around, they found their entryway had closed behind them, a massive stone slab sealing them in.

Panic welled up in Laila. "How did this happen? The door... it was open."

Ismail hurriedly approached the stone door, attempting to find a lever or mechanism. "These passages were designed with secrecy in mind. There must be a safety mechanism that triggered the closure. We need to find another way out."

The air grew cold, and the weight of their entrapment pressed on them. As minutes turned into hours, the limited oxygen and mounting fear threatened to overwhelm them.

Just as hope began to wane, a soft thud echoed from a distant corner of the chamber. Moments later, a faint glow approached, revealing the familiar face of Nasir.

"Nasir!" Laila exclaimed, relief evident in her voice.

He smiled, holding up a lantern. "I had a feeling you might need some guidance. The Mezquita's underground isn't kind to the uninitiated."

Ismail looked puzzled. "How did you know where to find us?"

Nasir chuckled, "I've explored these tunnels in my youth. When you didn't return after a while, I suspected you might've found the main chamber. And, as expected, got trapped."

He pointed to a section of the wall with a particular carving. Pressing it, another hidden door slid open, revealing a staircase leading upwards.

Laila, her gratitude evident, whispered, "Thank you, Nasir. We'd have been lost without you."

Nasir winked. "Every labyrinth has its minotaur. And every story, its guide."

As they ascended towards the Mezquita, the gravity of their adventure – and their narrow escape – began to sink in. The underground passages held secrets, but also dangers, and Laila realized that understanding the amulet's mystery would require more than just curiosity; it would need wisdom and caution.

***

Once back within the safety of the Mezquita's walls, Laila and Ismail found a secluded spot to catch their breath and review what they had seen in the underground chamber. Nasir, with his characteristic mysterious demeanor, had slipped away as quietly as he had appeared.

Laila carefully examined an artifact she had picked up from the underground chamber. It was an ornate scroll holder, adorned with geometric patterns typical of the era. Uncapping it, she carefully unrolled the aged parchment inside.

The writing, in an old script, detailed various rituals and ceremonies. While much of it was standard fare, a particular passage caught Laila's attention. It spoke of an annual ceremony where a sacred artifact, referred to only as "The Heart", would be presented to the city's most influential and noble families.

A small insignia was sketched beside this passage: a crescent moon with a star inside, enclosed by an intricate circle. It was a symbol Laila recognized immediately – it was the emblem of Kareem's family, a legacy that spanned centuries.

Ismail peered over her shoulder, his eyes narrowing at the insignia. "That's... that's the mark of Kareem's lineage."

Laila nodded. "This suggests that Kareem's ancestors were

directly involved with the rituals related to the amulet. It might explain his interest in the recent discoveries."

Ismail looked concerned. "But how does this relate to the skeleton or the hidden chamber? There's still so much we don't know."

Laila carefully rolled the scroll back and placed it in the holder. "While the connection isn't clear yet, one thing is: we need to speak with Kareem. He might hold the answers, or at least the next piece of the puzzle."

Ismail sighed, "Approaching Kareem won't be easy. But you're right; we need to know what he knows."

Laila tucked the scroll holder into her bag. "Tomorrow, we'll seek an audience with him. It's high time our paths converged."

As night descended upon Cordoba, Laila felt both apprehension and anticipation. The mystery of the amulet was unfolding, and she was determined to follow every lead, no matter where it took her.

8

Chapter 8

Cordoba was abuzz with anticipation. Kareem's parties were the stuff of legends, with grandeur that was spoken about for months. Guests arrived in their finest attire, each eager to partake in the evening's festivities. The courtyard of Kareem's palatial residence was transformed into a sea of silks and velvets, lit by countless lanterns casting a golden hue over the gathering.

Laila and Ismail, dressed in their best, entered the party cautiously. Every step they took was calculated, every conversation held with intent. They were on a mission, and amidst the revelry, they kept their wits about them.

Soft melodies played in the background, and dancers swirled to the rhythm, their moves as fluid as the waters of the ornate fountains dotted around the courtyard. Gourmet delicacies were served, filling the air with tantalizing aromas.

As the evening progressed, murmurs spread through the crowd about Kareem's promised surprise. Guests whispered, their speculations as varied as the stars in the night sky. And just when the anticipation was at its peak, a gong sounded, drawing all eyes to a raised platform at the courtyard's center.

Kareem, looking every bit the influential figure he was, stood confidently, a cloth-covered object beside him. "Esteemed guests," he began, his voice echoing through the vast space, "Thank you for gracing this evening with your presence. Tonight, I unveil a treasure, a piece of our city's glorious past."

With a dramatic flourish, he pulled away the cloth, revealing an intricately carved box. Opening it, he carefully lifted out a radiant gem, shimmering with an inner light that was almost ethereal. It was not the amulet, but its beauty was undeniable, and the gasps from the crowd were a testament to its allure.

"This gem," Kareem continued, "represents the heart of Cordoba, its legacy, and its future. It has been in my family for generations, passed down as a symbol of our lineage's commitment to this city."

Laila exchanged glances with Ismail. While the gem was undoubtedly mesmerizing, they both sensed there was more to Kareem's revelation than met the eye. This was not the amulet, but its unveiling at such a time, amidst the mysteries they were uncovering, couldn't be mere coincidence.

As the evening wore on, Laila knew their next move had to be a private audience with Kareem. The threads of the past were intertwining with the present, and the heart of the mystery seemed to beat louder with every passing moment.

***

The grandeur of the party continued, but there was an electric current of anticipation in the air. Laila and Ismail moved discreetly, working their way closer to Kareem, who was now surrounded by a circle of admirers, each eager to offer their compliments on the unveiled gem.

As Laila approached, she was intercepted by one of Kareem's trusted aides. "Lady Laila," he whispered, "Master Kareem requests your presence in the library."

Exchanging a look with Ismail, she followed the aide. The library was a testament to Kareem's wealth and knowledge. Shelves towered to the ceiling, filled with tomes and manuscripts from all over the known world.

Kareem stood by a large mahogany table, a velvet box open before him. As Laila entered, he looked up, his usually confident eyes showing a hint of vulnerability. "Laila," he began, "I've heard of your recent discoveries at the Mezquita, and I believe we share a common interest."

Opening the box, he revealed an amulet. It was remarkably similar to the one Laila had come across but had distinct markings setting it apart. The two pieces looked as if they were two halves of a whole.

"This has been in my family for generations," Kareem admitted. "It's said to have a twin, and legends speak of a vast treasure or power when the two are united."

Laila examined the amulet, her fingers tracing the intricate designs. "Why show this to me now?"

Kareem took a deep breath. "The legends also speak of a guardian, a protector of the twin amulets. I believe you might be that guardian. And with the events at the Mezquita, I think it's time for us to collaborate."

Laila raised an eyebrow. "What do you propose?"

"We pool our resources, share our knowledge, and together, we decipher the mystery of these amulets." Kareem's intensity was palpable. "I may have resources, Laila, but you have an intuition and understanding of history that is unparalleled."

Ismail, who had silently observed the exchange, finally spoke.

"This partnership could be beneficial, but how can we trust you?"

Kareem smiled ruefully, "Trust is earned, not given. But I hope my transparency tonight is a start."

Laila considered Kareem's words and the weight of the amulet in her hands. The puzzle was becoming more complex, but with Kareem's involvement, they might be closer to solving it.

"Alright," Laila finally said, "we collaborate. But every step is taken together."

Kareem nodded, sealing their new alliance, as outside, the party continued in blissful ignorance of the intrigue unfolding within the walls of the library.

***

After the intense discussion in the library, Laila found a quiet balcony overlooking Kareem's expansive gardens. The cool night air was a soothing balm, allowing her to gather her thoughts. Ismail joined her, leaning against the balustrade.

"You seem troubled," he observed, handing her a cup of mint tea.

Laila took a deep sip, letting the warmth spread through her. "I am. Aligning with Kareem, even for a noble cause, is not without risks. He is influential, and while he seems genuine now, power and wealth can often cloud one's judgment."

Ismail nodded, understanding her reservations. "But Laila, you've always been one to prioritize history, legacy, and the greater good over personal reservations."

She smiled faintly, "I know. That's the crux of my turmoil. If this alliance can unlock the mysteries of Cordoba's past and bring to light stories lost in time, isn't it worth the risk?"

"The question is," Ismail responded, "are you prepared for what we might uncover? The tale of these amulets is entwined with legends, power struggles, and perhaps, even darker secrets."

Laila looked at the night sky, stars twinkling like distant beacons of hope. "Every era has its stories, its guardians. Perhaps it's our duty now to ensure these tales don't remain buried."

Ismail took her hand, offering silent support. "We're in this together. As always."

With a resolute nod, Laila replied, "For the sake of history, for Cordoba, we'll embark on this journey with Kareem. But we tread cautiously, with our eyes and ears open."

Their decision made, the duo rejoined the party, mingling with the guests. But now, there was a newfound determination in Laila's steps, a spark in her eyes. The guardian of Cordoba's tales was on a mission, and she would see it through to the end, come what may.

9

Chapter 9

The morning after the party, Laila and Ismail arrived at Kareem's residence, their purpose clear. The grand doors opened to reveal a more subdued setting than the previous night. The remnants of the lavish gathering were all but gone, replaced by a sense of anticipation.

They were ushered into a spacious study. Rich tapestries adorned the walls, and the room was bathed in a soft, natural light from the large windows. Kareem stood by a vast table, spread with maps, manuscripts, and tools.

"Welcome," he greeted, though his usual commanding demeanor seemed slightly muted. "I hope last night's revelations have given you some insight into my intentions."

Laila replied cautiously, "Revelations are one thing, Kareem. Trust is another."

Kareem nodded, acknowledging her point. "Agreed. But our shared goal is larger than any misgivings. These amulets have been separated for centuries. We are uniquely positioned to piece together their story."

Ismail looked at the maps, his fingers brushing over the

ancient papers. "Where do we begin?"

Kareem gestured to a scroll, its edges frayed with age. "This mentions the two amulets and hints at their origin. But it's written in a cryptic language, and my scholars have struggled with it."

Laila's eyes lit up with recognition. "I've come across this before, during my studies. It's a mix of old Andalusian script with some ancient symbols. It will take time, but with combined efforts, we can decipher it."

As the trio bent over the scroll, there was a palpable sense of shared purpose. But underlying that was a tension, the knowledge that each brought their own motives and secrets to the table.

Hours passed, the room filled with discussions, debates, and the occasional disagreement. Slowly, the text began to reveal its secrets, pointing to locations, dates, and ceremonies.

By late afternoon, they had a rough roadmap, a path that would guide their search for answers. But as they stepped back to assess their progress, it was clear that the alliance, while productive, was still tenuous.

Ismail voiced what they all felt, "This partnership will only work if we're transparent with each other. No secrets, no hidden agendas."

Kareem met his gaze, "Agreed. We're united in purpose, if not in trust. But give it time. Perhaps we'll surprise each other."

Laila, ever the peacemaker, intervened, "For now, let's focus on the task at hand. The story of the amulets awaits, and we are its narrators."

And with that, the unlikely trio embarked on their shared journey, each step into the past fraught with challenges, yet holding the promise of historic revelations.

***

The door to Kareem's study opened gently, but the trio was so engrossed in their work that they didn't notice Yasmine's silent entrance. She hesitated for a moment, clutching a piece of ornate fabric in her hand. Taking a deep breath, she stepped forward.

"Laila, I thought this might be of interest," Yasmine began hesitantly, her voice low but assertive.

Laila looked up, surprise evident on her face. "Yasmine? What brings you here?"

Yasmine unfurled the piece of fabric, revealing an intricate pattern. "I found this in my grandmother's chest. She used to tell me tales of a cloth woven with the stories of old Cordoba, stories that were handed down from generation to generation."

Laila approached, her historian's instinct piqued. The fabric was old, the threads worn, but the patterns were vivid. There were shapes and symbols similar to the ones on the scroll they'd been deciphering. And at the center, two identical amulet patterns, almost as if they were drawn by someone who had seen them firsthand.

Ismail squinted at the design. "This...this looks like a map! See these symbols? They correlate to old landmarks."

Kareem, usually composed, looked visibly shocked. "This fabric might be the key. If it's a map, it could lead us to the origin of the amulets or perhaps even the rumored treasure."

Laila was quick to connect the dots. "The symbols on this fabric, combined with the deciphered scroll, could give us a clearer direction."

Yasmine watched the excitement unfold, a hint of pride in her eyes. "Grandmother always said the cloth held magic. That it had a story to tell. I guess she was right."

Kareem approached Yasmine, gratitude evident in his demeanor. "This contribution is invaluable. You've brought us closer to solving a mystery that has eluded many."

Laila smiled, placing a reassuring hand on Yasmine's shoulder. "Your grandmother's legacy lives on through you. Together, we'll unravel the story she cherished."

As the group huddled around the table, placing the fabric alongside the ancient scroll, the patterns began to weave a clearer narrative, guiding them deeper into Cordoba's enigmatic past.

***

The study dimmed as evening approached, the soft golden glow from the lamps highlighting the ancient patterns on the fabric. Laila, Kareem, and Ismail had spread the cloth out, using the scroll to cross-reference symbols, while Yasmine provided context from her grandmother's tales.

"These wavy lines," Ismail traced them with his fingers, "they have to be a depiction of the Guadalquivir River. And see this mark here? It's positioned where the old Roman bridge would be."

Laila nodded in agreement. "I think you're onto something. The river played a central role in many ancient tales. It was the heart of Cordoba, with many secrets buried along its banks."

Kareem leaned in closer, "There's a sequence. First, the depiction of the Mezquita, then the river, and then this..." he pointed at a star-like emblem, "which from our deciphering earlier, signifies a gathering point or a place of significance."

Yasmine chimed in, recalling one of her grandmother's tales,

"She spoke of the 'Star of the River', a location where poets, scholars, and mystics would meet, share stories, and hide treasures for safekeeping. I always thought it was a metaphor."

Laila's eyes widened in realization. "No, it's not a metaphor. It's a confluence! Where the old streams met the river. The 'Star of the River' could be a literal point on the Guadalquivir."

Ismail quickly sketched out the layout of the river as they knew it, marking the probable confluence points. "One of these has to be our 'Star'. The amulets, when combined, might hold more significance at this point."

Kareem looked thoughtful. "We need to be careful. If this is indeed a treasure point, it might be guarded or watched. The last thing we want is to alert others before we unveil the mystery."

Laila packed up the fabric and scroll carefully. "Tomorrow at dawn, we'll start our exploration of the river. The 'Star of the River' awaits, and with it, the next chapter of our tale."

As the trio parted ways for the night, the shimmering waters of the Guadalquivir held promise, secrets, and the echoes of a history long waiting to be uncovered.

10

Chapter 10

The first light of dawn painted the Guadalquivir in hues of gold and azure. Laila, Kareem, and Ismail met by the riverbank, their boat equipped with ropes, lanterns, and tools that would assist them in their underwater exploration.

Laila adjusted her attire, preparing for the exploration. "According to the fabric's pattern, the 'Star of the River' should be at the confluence right ahead."

Ismail took the helm, navigating the boat smoothly. "Remember, the river has changed over centuries. While the confluence point remains, the landmarks and surroundings may have shifted."

As they approached the predicted location, Kareem took out a small, ornate diving bell, an ancient tool used for underwater exploration. "This will help one of us explore the riverbed, while the others stay on the boat to ensure safety."

Laila volunteered, "I'm the smallest and lightest. I should go. Plus, I've had some experience with these."

Securing herself and taking a deep breath, Laila was lowered into the water, the bell providing her with precious air. As she descended, the world transformed. The muffled sounds of the river's currents whispered ancient tales, and the refracted sunlight unveiled a mosaic of submerged artifacts.

Laila's heart raced as she spotted a series of strategically placed stones on the riverbed, forming a pattern eerily similar to the amulet's design. The stones led her to an ancient, sealed clay jar, half-buried beneath the silt.

Using her tools, Laila carefully extricated the jar and signaled to be pulled up. As she broke the water's surface, her excitement was palpable.

"We've found something," she exclaimed, holding up the mud-caked jar.

Ismail and Kareem hurriedly helped her onboard. Wiping away the grime, they discovered inscriptions on the jar. It looked like a continuation of the story they were piecing together.

Kareem, his voice shaking with anticipation, said, "The river has kept its secret for centuries. Today, we begin to unravel it."

With the ancient artifact in hand and the promise of more clues within, the trio headed back to the shore, their bond strengthened by the shared adventure and the weight of the discovery they had just made.

***

As the boat approached the bank, the trio noticed a lone figure waiting. Cloaked in a rich, flowing robe, Rima stood with an air of expectation. Her posture and piercing gaze made it evident that she had been following their progress.

Kareem was the first to step off the boat, securing it and casting a wary eye at Rima. "What brings you here at this hour?"

Rima stepped forward, her voice dripping with an enticing mix of charm and menace. "Why, the same thing that brings you here, dear cousin. Curiosity... and perhaps the glint of gold?"

Laila tightened her grip on the clay jar, ready to defend their find. "This is a historical artifact, Rima. Not some trinket to be bartered."

Rima laughed softly, "Ah, dear Laila, always the scholar. But did you ever wonder why this 'artifact' was hidden away? Maybe there's more than just historical significance."

Ismail, ever the peacemaker, tried to diffuse the tension. "We're all after the truth here. Perhaps we can collaborate?"

Rima smirked, revealing a small parchment from her robe. "I have this – an old poem from Hana's collection. It hints at the dual nature of the treasure. Part history, part... something more powerful. And I believe that jar," she gestured towards the clay container, "holds the key."

Kareem sighed, "Why didn't you come to us directly? Why the veiled threats?"

Rima looked away, her demeanor softening momentarily, "Because, cousin, I've debts that need settling. Powerful people, who don't care for history but for power. The treasure, or the secret it holds, could be my salvation."

Laila, sensing the genuine desperation in Rima's voice, approached her. "We can help you, Rima, but not if you work against us."

Rima took a deep breath, weighing her choices. "Alright. But we must act quickly. If the stories are true, and this treasure wields power, we're not the only ones who will be seeking it."

The group, now larger by one, looked at the sealed jar. Its contents held the power to change their destinies, and they knew their journey was only beginning.

***

The night had darkened considerably. As the group deliberated their next move, a sudden rush of footsteps from the surrounding woods interrupted their conversation. The trees seemed to come alive with shadows, as figures cloaked in darkness emerged, trapping them in a semi-circle.

A deep voice rang out, "Hand over the jar, and no one gets hurt."

Rima muttered under her breath, "Too late. They're here."

Before anyone could react, a volley of arrows flew from a hidden spot, hitting the ground in front of the assailants and creating a smoke screen. Taking advantage of the momentary chaos, Ismail yelled, "Run!"

The group scattered, Laila clutching the jar close to her chest as she navigated the forest, relying on her knowledge of the local terrain.

As she rounded a bend, she came face-to-face with Commander Rashid, his stern expression illuminated by the dim moonlight.

"Laila," he breathed, his tone revealing a mix of relief and frustration. "Do you realize the trouble you've caused?"

Laila, panting, replied, "Commander Rashid, this isn't what it looks like. We're trying to protect history, not steal it."

Rashid sheathed his sword and moved closer, "Every whisper in Cordoba speaks of a treasure, of power. And now, people are willing to kill for it. Your exploration has awakened old, sleeping beasts."

Laila looked down at the jar, "But we can't just bury the past again. The truth needs to come out."

Commander Rashid sighed, "And it will, but in due time. For

now, let the authorities handle this."

Laila hesitated. "I can't just hand this over. Not when we're so close."

Rashid's eyes softened, "I give you my word, as a commander and as a friend of your father's, I'll ensure its safety. But right now, you need to be safe. Let's get you out of here."

As they began their way back to Cordoba, the weight of the situation pressed heavily on Laila. The intertwined paths of history, power, and ambition were proving to be more complex and dangerous than she had ever imagined.

11

Chapter 11

The sun had just begun its ascent, casting the city in a warm, golden glow. Commander Rashid's quarters, located within the fortress overseeing Cordoba, were adorned with artifacts and scrolls that reflected his position and intellect.

Laila, determined and steadfast, stood facing Rashid across a large wooden table, the clay jar placed between them.

"Commander," she began, her voice firm, "this isn't just about a treasure or its rumored power. It's about Cordoba, our history, and the legacy we leave behind."

Rashid, leaning back, folded his arms, his expression inscrutable. "You put yourself at great risk, Laila. For what? A story?"

Laila leaned in, placing a hand on the jar. "Not just any story. A story that has been buried, forgotten, and now seeks to be told. This," she pointed at the jar, "might be a piece of our past that could shape our future."

She continued, "The same whispers you spoke of last night? They're not just of greed. There are those genuinely interested in the truth, like me."

Rashid exhaled slowly, "It's not about trust, Laila. It's about ensuring peace in the city. What if this truth causes chaos?"

Laila, her eyes bright with conviction, countered, "But what if it brings unity? Closure? A shared heritage that's been lost?"

There was a momentary silence as the weight of her words settled.

Rashid spoke, softer this time, "Your father, he too was passionate about our history. I see the same fire in you. But passion can sometimes blind judgment."

Laila's voice quivered, "I know the risks. But with your guidance and the protection of the city's forces, we can unravel this mystery the right way."

Rashid stared at her for what felt like an eternity. Finally, he nodded, "Alright. But on one condition. We do this together, and at any sign of trouble, we pull back."

Laila's eyes glistened with tears of gratitude, "Agreed."

As they shook hands, sealing their new alliance, the sun shone brighter, casting away the shadows of doubt. The journey ahead was uncertain, but with Commander Rashid by her side, Laila felt invigorated and ready to face the challenges that lay ahead.

***

The grand arches of the Mezquita seemed even more impressive as Laila, Commander Rashid, and Farida stepped into its cool confines. The hushed whispers of the past seemed to echo through its corridors, as if the very walls were alive with stories.

Farida, her aged eyes reflecting a lifetime of wisdom, gestured for them to follow. "There's an area few venture into. Old tales speak of sacred spaces and rituals from times long past."

They wound their way through the forest of pillars, their

footsteps muffled by the ancient stone. Commander Rashid's sharp eyes darted around, ever vigilant, while Laila hung on Farida's every word.

Soon, they reached a secluded corner, dominated by an intricately carved mihrab that glittered in the dim light. The niche was flanked by forgotten rooms, sealed for centuries.

Farida gestured at the mihrab, "Legend speaks of a parallel chamber, mirroring this one but hidden. A place of worship and secret gatherings."

Laila looked around, her historian's instincts kicking in. "But where? There's no indication of another chamber."

Rashid, kneeling, examined the floor's mosaic patterns, tracing them with his fingers. "Patterns often hold keys." He pressed down on a particular tile, and with a soft grinding noise, part of the adjacent wall shifted, revealing a narrow passageway.

Farida smiled, "The old tales did not lie."

The passage led them to a chamber mirroring the one they had just left, but this one was untouched by time. Dust hung thick in the air, and the remnants of old parchments, pottery, and artifacts lay scattered about. At its center stood another mihrab, its walls etched with intricate patterns and scripts.

Laila, her heart racing, approached it. "This script... it's ancient. Pre-Islamic. It speaks of a union, of two worlds coming together."

Farida nodded, "This chamber was likely a meeting point for leaders and scholars of different faiths, a testament to the city's harmonious past."

Rashid, examining a dusty scroll, mused, "This could provide the context we need to understand the treasure's significance."

Laila, looking at the artifacts, felt a profound connection to her ancestors. "We're standing where they stood, seeing what they saw. It's... overwhelming."

Farida placed a comforting hand on Laila's shoulder, "History is a living entity, dear. You're not just exploring it; you're becoming a part of it."

As they began cataloging the findings, the chamber's significance became evident. It wasn't just about treasures or power; it was a testament to a time when Cordoba was a beacon of knowledge, tolerance, and unity. A message from the past, with profound implications for the future.

***

Laila's fingers brushed against a scroll when a small, flat piece of metal fell out, landing on the stone floor with a soft clang. She picked it up, revealing a bronze plaque covered in intricate engravings.

Rashid, noticing the plaque, squinted at the design. "It looks like a combination of scripts – Arabic, Hebrew, and even Visigothic runes."

Farida leaned in, her fingers tracing the words, "This is a convergence of cultures. But these aren't just random words. It's a riddle."

Laila, her eyes lighting up, read aloud:

"By the light of Luna, where waters run deep,
Where the faithful kneel, and wise men seek,
Three pillars stand, and in their keep,
Rests Cordoba's heart, in eternal sleep."

Rashid's brow furrowed in thought. "It's clearly referring to a location in Cordoba, but what and where?"

Laila pondered, "The mention of Luna could refer to the moon or maybe a reflection in the Guadalquivir River. And the faithful kneeling... the Mezquita itself?"

Farida added, "And three pillars could be literal pillars, or figuratively the three cultures: Muslim, Jewish, and Christian."

Rashid held up the plaque towards the light filtering in from the chamber's entrance. "Look closely. See these notches around the edge? They may indicate a specific alignment."

Laila's eyes widened in realization. "An alignment with the pillars! If we position ourselves correctly in the Mezquita during a specific phase of the moon..."

Farida nodded, "We might reveal the next clue or the location of this treasure, Cordoba's heart."

Rashid, rolling up the scrolls they had discovered, stated, "Then we need to decode this fully, ensure our interpretation is correct. We must approach this with both respect and caution."

Laila, clutching the plaque, felt a surge of anticipation. "This isn't just about riches. It's about a symbol of unity, an artifact that represents the golden age of Cordoba."

Farida smiled gently, "And you, Laila, are the bridge to rediscovering it."

As they left the chamber, the weight of their discovery pressed upon them. This was bigger than a mere treasure hunt; it was a journey into the heart of a city and its legacy.

12

Chapter 12

The Mezquita was abuzz with anticipation. Word had spread of the discoveries, and a grand assembly had been called. The golden mosaics shimmered, reflecting the light from numerous lanterns placed strategically around the vast prayer hall. The gentle hum of whispered conversations filled the air.

Laila, her attire reflecting the gravity of the occasion, stood near the grand mihrab, taking in the sight. The prominent families of Cordoba, scholars, city officials, and even intrigued commonfolk were present. It was a gathering the likes of which hadn't been seen in a long while.

Commander Rashid, in his ceremonial uniform, was in deep conversation with Majid, the treasurer. Yasmine and Farida stood together, exchanging notes, while Ismail and Kareem, in a rare moment, seemed to be on cordial terms, discussing the intricacies of the recently discovered chamber.

Hana, the poetess, was reciting soft verses to an enthralled group, her words weaving tales of ancient glory and secrets buried deep. Nearby, Nasir animatedly explained the underground passages to a group of young scholars, his hands mimicking the maze beneath.

Zaid, with his old scripts, was surrounded by a group of eager listeners, while Rima, draped in her finest silks, watched the proceedings with a hawk-eyed interest, her motivations as always, a mystery.

Laila cleared her throat, calling for attention. The murmurs died down as all eyes turned to her.

"Esteemed guests," she began, her voice echoing confidently, "We stand today on the precipice of rediscovering a piece of our history. A legacy that celebrates the confluence of our cultures."

She displayed the bronze plaque. "This riddle is a testament to the unity of Cordoba. As we delve deeper, I urge everyone to remember that this isn't about personal gains but about honoring our shared heritage."

Rashid stepped forward, "The city's forces are at your disposal. We will ensure that this quest remains honorable and true to its purpose."

Kareem, not to be outdone, added, "And the resources of my family will aid in this endeavor."

Laila nodded appreciatively, "With such unity, we're bound to succeed. Let's come together, decipher the clues, and unveil the treasures of our past."

As the assembly broke into smaller groups, discussing theories and sharing insights, the Mezquita, with its grand arches and pillars, seemed to approve. For within its walls, the spirit of unity and discovery was rekindled, echoing the glory days of Cordoba.

***

In a quieter corner of the Mezquita, Laila set up a makeshift

59

research area. Scrolls and books were laid out on an intricately woven carpet, and a lantern cast a warm glow, creating a serene ambiance amidst the larger assembly's excitement.

Zaid joined her, offering a script he believed might assist. "I've seen a similar riddle in this text," he murmured, handing over a fragile-looking parchment.

Laila, with careful hands, began comparing the riddle on the plaque with the script's annotations. Hours seemed to melt away as words, numbers, and symbols were dissected and aligned.

Farida, Yasmine, and Ismail occasionally provided insights, while Nasir mapped out potential physical locations within the Mezquita. Rima, seemingly out of sheer curiosity, hovered on the periphery, listening intently.

Finally, a breakthrough.

Laila's fingers traced the phrase in the old script that matched the riddle's essence: "*The heart lies where the moon's glow meets the fountain's echo.*"

Yasmine's eyes lit up in recognition. "The Court of the Lions! It has a fountain that echoes the surroundings. And during a particular moon phase, its reflection perfectly aligns with the lion statues."

Ismail added, "Yes, and it's said the fountain was constructed as a homage to an even older artifact. Perhaps that's where the relic is hidden."

Laila nodded in agreement. "The riddle speaks of Luna's light, the moon's reflection, aligning with the fountain's echo. When the moonlight hits a specific spot, it might reveal the relic."

Rashid, having overheard the conversation, remarked, "The next full moon is in two days. We should prepare and be vigilant."

Farida, her gaze distant, whispered, "It's said that the relic was a symbol of unity, gifted to Cordoba during its golden age. It's not just a treasure; it embodies the spirit of the city."

Rima, her voice laced with intrigue, added, "And such a relic could hold power, not just historical significance."

Laila, clutching the bronze plaque, felt the gravity of their discovery. "In two days, we'll not only uncover a treasure but also a testament to Cordoba's legacy. We must ensure it remains protected and honored."

As the group dispersed, making preparations for the imminent revelation, the Mezquita's shadows seemed to dance, as if in anticipation of an age-old secret finally coming to light.

***

As the assembly continued, a soft melody floated through the air. It was Hana, seated gracefully by a pillar, her voice weaving tales of love, valor, and mystery. The audience around her was rapt, lost in the beauty of her prose.

Laila, taking a moment from her research, joined the crowd to listen. However, her respite was short-lived. As Hana began reciting a poem about the moon's secrets, there was a sudden commotion from the entrance of the Mezquita.

A group of masked men, their faces obscured by dark cloaks, stormed into the space. The assembly scattered in panic, and in the ensuing chaos, two of the intruders grabbed Hana, muffling her protests with a swift, expert move.

Laila, recognizing the danger, yelled out, "Stop them!" But the assailants were quick, disappearing amidst the columns and arches of the Mezquita.

Rashid, drawing his sword and rallying a group of guards, shouted, "Secure the exits!" But the intruders seemed to know the Mezquita's intricate layout too well and managed to evade capture.

Ismail, breathless from a failed chase, returned to Laila's side. "They were too fast, and they knew exactly whom they wanted."

Kareem, his face a mix of anger and worry, added, "But why Hana? She's a poetess, not a player in this game of treasures and relics."

Farida, her voice shaking, whispered, "Perhaps her poetry holds clues or secrets that we aren't aware of. Or maybe they believe she knows more than she's revealed."

Yasmine, her eyes filled with tears, cried, "We have to save her. She's innocent in all of this."

Rima, surprisingly, was the first to take control. "Mourn and worry later. Act now. We need to find her."

Rashid, ever the commander, ordered, "Double the patrols. Interview everyone. Someone must've seen something."

Laila, her heart heavy but her resolve firm, said, "We need to decode the riddle, find the relic, and save Hana. They're all connected. We're running out of time."

As the assembly regrouped, the Mezquita, a silent witness to centuries of events, echoed with a mix of fear, determination, and hope. The search for the relic had taken a personal and dangerous turn, and Laila knew they were now playing a high-stakes game.

13

Chapter 13

The Mezquita was a hive of activity, but Laila found a quiet corner to strategize. She knew they had very little time. Every moment Hana remained in the hands of the kidnappers, the stakes grew higher.

Rashid was the first to join her. "I've sent my best guards to search every nook and cranny of Cordoba. They won't rest until Hana is found."

Laila nodded in appreciation. "But we need to think beyond just manpower. These kidnappers knew the Mezquita well and took Hana for a reason. We need information, and we need allies."

Farida, her wisdom evident, suggested, "The scholars and librarians of the city. They're a network of knowledge. If there's a secret Hana tapped into, they might be aware."

Kareem, usually more reserved, was assertive. "I've contacts in the merchant world. They hear whispers, see movements. I'll have them on the lookout for anything unusual."

Ismail, determination in his eyes, said, "The builders and architects who've worked on the Mezquita's restorations over the years. They would know the city's secrets, its underground passages. I'll rally them."

Laila was touched by the outpouring of support. "Then there's the public. Hana has touched many lives with her poetry. They could be our eyes and ears."

Yasmine, taking a deep breath, offered, "I can rally the women. We have our own networks, especially in the markets. No one sees or hears more than the women of Cordoba."

Rima, her motives still a mystery but her skills undeniable, whispered, "I know people in the shadows. They owe me favors. I'll have them watch the darker corners of the city."

Laila, inspired by the collective determination, declared, "This isn't just about a relic or a riddle anymore. It's about one of our own, and the spirit of Cordoba. Together, we're formidable. Let's bring Hana home."

As the group dispersed, each with their task, the Mezquita echoed with renewed energy. It was a race against time, but with a united Cordoba, hope reigned supreme.

***

Word had quickly spread that suspicious activity was noted at the ancient ruins outside Cordoba. Historically, these were remnants of an older civilization, often used as a meeting spot for clandestine gatherings due to its relative isolation from the city's hustle and bustle.

Ismail had received this tip from one of the architects who had worked near the area. Without wasting any time, Laila, Rashid, Ismail, and a group of guards, aided by Rima's shadowy contacts, made their way towards the ruins.

The moon cast an eerie glow over the broken pillars and

archways. Every echo seemed amplified, and the night was thick with anticipation.

Laila, her senses heightened, felt the electric charge in the air. "We need to tread carefully. They could be watching."

Rashid, his hand resting on the hilt of his sword, whispered, "Spread out. Signal if you see anything."

As the group dispersed amongst the ruins, a soft melody floated towards Laila. It was unmistakably Hana's voice. Following the sound, Laila and Ismail stumbled upon an underground chamber, cleverly hidden beneath overgrown vegetation.

Peeking through a small crack, they saw Hana, bound but defiant, reciting her poetry, perhaps to keep her spirits up. Surrounding her were the masked kidnappers, their attention on a rugged-looking individual who seemed to be their leader.

Rima, blending seamlessly with the shadows, joined Laila and Ismail. "That's Haroun. He's an artifact smuggler, known for trading historical treasures for gold in foreign lands."

Laila, realizing the gravity of the situation, said, "He's not just after the relic. He wants the lore, the history, and Hana is his key to deciphering it."

Ismail, spotting a potential escape route, whispered, "We need a diversion. We can't confront them head-on; they're too many."

Rima, with a glint in her eye, murmured, "Leave the diversion to me." She swiftly disappeared, only to reappear moments later on the other side of the ruins, setting off a series of bright flares.

The kidnappers were momentarily blinded and disoriented by the sudden burst of light. Seizing the opportunity, Rashid and the guards stormed the chamber. A brief but intense skirmish ensued. Laila, using the element of surprise, freed Hana.

As the dust settled, the kidnappers were overpowered, and

Haroun was captured. Rima, her face hidden beneath her cloak, gave a nod of acknowledgment to Laila.

With Hana safely rescued, the ruins, once symbols of a forgotten past, had borne witness to a battle for Cordoba's future. The city's history, it seemed, was both its vulnerability and its strength.

*****

Back at the safety of the Mezquita, Hana was quickly attended to by Yasmine and Farida, who provided her with fresh clothes and a comforting elixir to soothe her nerves.

Laila, her emotions a whirlwind of relief and anger, turned her attention to the captured Haroun, now bound and watched closely by Rashid's guards.

With the moonlight streaming through the open courtyard, Laila approached the smuggler. "Why Hana? What did you hope to gain by kidnapping a poetess?"

Haroun, his arrogance undiminished by his capture, sneered, "You still don't see, do you? It's not about gold or treasures. It's about power. Knowledge is power, and history, tales, lore... they're all keys to that power."

Hana, her voice firm despite her ordeal, added, "He wanted me to decipher an old poetic script, one that's believed to reveal the location of an ancient artifact. My family passed down these verses through generations, but their meaning was lost to time."

Rima, ever mysterious, remarked, "And yet, Haroun, you underestimated Cordoba. You believed our history was for sale."

Rashid, his patience thinning, interjected, "What did you intend to do with this artifact?"

Haroun chuckled, "It's a symbol, Commander. In the right

hands, it's a claim, a statement. The one who possesses it can sway the will of many."

Ismail realized, "You intended to manipulate the masses, rewrite history, and position yourself as a powerful influencer."

Haroun's smirk confirmed Ismail's suspicion. Laila, however, had one more question. "Who's backing you, Haroun? Who else seeks this power?"

Haroun leaned in, whispering, "Guess you'll have to find out."

His cryptic response hinted at a larger game in play, one that was far from over. The night, while victorious for Laila and her friends, was also a revelation: the true battle for Cordoba's soul had only just begun.

14

Chapter 14

After Haroun's revelation, Laila couldn't rest. With Hana's knowledge and the clues they had gathered, the group felt they were closer than ever to finding the elusive artifact. Based on the poetic verses Hana had been forced to interpret, the search led them to an old section of the Mezquita, long sealed off from the public.

With Farida's sage knowledge, Ismail's architectural expertise, and Laila's determination, they finally located a hidden chamber. It was sealed with an ancient lock, its design corresponding to the twin amulets they had found earlier.

Laila fitted the amulets into the lock, and with a soft click, the chamber doors creaked open. The room was bathed in a soft, ethereal light filtering through cracks in the ceiling. In the center stood a pedestal, upon which rested a chest intricately carved with geometric patterns and verses from the Quran.

Laila approached it with reverence. As she opened the chest, the group found no gold, jewels, or any tangible treasures. Instead, there were scrolls, aged but preserved, filled with writings.

Farida, her hands trembling with emotion, recognized the scripts. "These are teachings lost to time, philosophies and interpretations of life, science, and spirituality from great scholars of the past."

Hana, her eyes scanning the scrolls, whispered, "These verses... they resonate with the ones passed down in my family. They speak of unity, understanding, and the quest for knowledge."

Ismail, visibly moved, remarked, "It's not wealth, but wisdom. A treasure that can truly elevate Cordoba and its people."

Rashid, with a newfound respect for the city's legacy, added, "Haroun and whoever backs him sought power, but true power lies in enlightening the masses, not manipulating them."

Laila, holding a scroll, realized the weight of their discovery. "We've uncovered not just Cordoba's history but its soul. This knowledge could usher in a new era of prosperity and enlightenment."

The chamber, silent for centuries, echoed with the group's determination to share these teachings, ensuring that Cordoba's legacy was not just in its past but would shape its future.

***

After the profound discovery in the Mezquita's hidden chamber, the group gathered in a more private location to discuss their next steps. The intricate salon of Farida's home was chosen, with its walls lined with books and artifacts bearing witness to their deliberations.

As they settled in, Rima stepped forward, her usual air of mystery replaced by an uncharacteristic vulnerability. "There's something I must confess," she began, her voice barely above a whisper.

Laila, still recalling their recent alliance, prompted her to continue. "Speak freely, Rima."

With a deep breath, Rima revealed, "I was once involved with Haroun, not romantically, but as partners in the shadowy trade of artifacts. I believed it was a way to reclaim our history, but I soon realized his motives were not as noble as mine."

Rashid's gaze intensified. "Why didn't you reveal this before?"

Rima looked down, guilt evident in her eyes. "I wanted out, but he had something over me. Blackmail. It was only when I saw Laila's passion for Cordoba's true history that I realized I had to make amends."

As the weight of her confession hung in the air, the door creaked open. Kareem stepped in, the twin amulet dangling from his fingers.

Laila's eyes narrowed. "Why are you here, Kareem?"

He sighed, "Not as an enemy, but as someone who too was led astray by ambition. The amulet was passed down in my family. I sought its pair, thinking it would lead me to wealth. But after seeing what we've uncovered, I understand its true value."

Farida, ever the wise observer, inquired, "What do you intend to do now?"

Kareem looked at the scrolls Laila held. "I wish to support its dissemination. Use my resources to ensure this knowledge reaches every corner of Cordoba and beyond."

Laila, recalling the distrust she once held for him, saw sincerity in his eyes. "Then let's ensure Cordoba's legacy shines, not as a beacon of wealth, but as a lighthouse of wisdom."

The room, once thick with tension, now resonated with newfound alliances and a shared purpose. The paths of Rima and

Kareem, though fraught with past misdeeds, had converged with those committed to Cordoba's true essence. The next chapter for Cordoba awaited, and they were ready to write it.

***

Word quickly spread throughout Cordoba about the astonishing discovery. The city's bustling streets, usually alive with trade and gossip, were now abuzz with anticipation for the grand unveiling of the sacred scrolls.

The central plaza of the Mezquita was chosen for the event. Majestic banners floated down from its archways, adorned with quotes from the newly discovered teachings, casting their enlightened shadow upon the masses below. Musicians played soft Andalusian tunes, filling the air with a sense of festivity and reverence.

In the center, a grand podium was erected. Upon it, the chest containing the sacred scrolls stood, guarded by Commander Rashid and his men, a symbol of the city's renewed commitment to its heritage.

Laila stood at the podium, her heart heavy with the weight of the moment. Beside her were Farida, Ismail, Yasmine, and others who had played a part in the discovery. Even Kareem and a redeemed Rima were present, standing shoulder to shoulder with the rest.

Addressing the vast crowd, Laila began, "Today is not just a day of celebration but a day of reawakening. What we've found is not mere parchment and ink, but the soul of Cordoba."

She gestured to the chest, "This isn't a treasure to be hoarded, but knowledge to be shared. To be studied, understood, and applied."

As she spoke, scholars from the city's famed institutions stepped forward, ready to transcribe and distribute the teachings.

Kareem, taking a moment to address the assembly, announced, "I pledge to fund centers of learning across Cordoba where these teachings will be made available to all, regardless of their social standing."

Rima, with a nod from Laila, stepped forward and recited a poem, a blend of Hana's verses and the ancient scrolls' wisdom, encapsulating the spirit of the day.

As the sun began to set, casting the Mezquita in a golden hue, the citizens of Cordoba gathered around the sacred relic, reading, discussing, and embracing their rediscovered heritage. The city, once a melting pot of cultures, was once again at the forefront of a new era of enlightenment, unity, and progress.

15

Chapter 15

The rhythmic pattern of daily life in Cordoba had a new energy. The sun seemed to shine brighter, the streets hummed with renewed vigor, and everywhere you turned, there were signs of the city's recent revelation.

In the heart of the city, the market thrived. Instead of the usual bickering over prices and quality, merchants and customers exchanged pleasantries, snippets from the newly discovered teachings, and heartfelt stories inspired by them.

At a corner of the marketplace, Yasmine's fabric stall drew a considerable crowd. The intricate patterns of her textiles, now inspired by the teachings, were becoming a favorite among the citizens. Ismail stopped by, offering gentle suggestions on preserving the architectural essence of Cordoba in her designs.

Naima's apothecary, next to Yasmine's stall, had a new sign which read: "Healing the body and the soul." Her potions now came with quotes from the scrolls, weaving together the art of physical healing with spiritual enlightenment.

Laila, walking through the market, couldn't help but smile at the change around her. She met Zaid, who enthusiastically showed her a new script he was working on, inspired by the ancient verses. Ahmed recounted tales that echoed the wisdom of the scrolls to eager listeners around his stall.

The Alcazar gardens, usually a quiet retreat, now hosted scholars, poets, and thinkers. They gathered in groups, discussing, debating, and imbibing the essence of the ancient teachings. Farida led many of these discussions, her vast knowledge now paired with the newfound teachings.

As the sun dipped, casting the city in a warm, amber glow, Hana's voice echoed from the Mezquita's minaret. Her evening poetry, blending the old with the new, became a symbol of the city's transformed spirit.

Through every alley, square, and corner, there was a palpable sense of camaraderie. Past conflicts seemed trivial, old grudges faded, and the citizens of Cordoba were united, not just by their shared history, but by the hope and wisdom of a brighter future.

***

The grand courtyard of the Mezquita, with its mesmerizing row of arches and serene ambience, had always been a place of reflection for Laila. Amidst the harmonious interplay of light and shadow, she found a quiet nook, settling down with a few scattered scrolls and her journal.

She wrote about the profound changes she'd witnessed in Cordoba, the challenges faced, alliances forged, and the rediscovery of a spiritual treasure. However, as she penned down her experiences, her thoughts began drifting towards the future.

Laila pondered the vast world outside Cordoba. The scrolls had hinted at connections far beyond the city's boundaries, with references to distant lands and civilizations. While Cordoba had been the heart of this story, the veins of history stretched out in all directions, and Laila felt a growing urge to trace them.

She scribbled a list in her journal:

1. *The Byzantine Enigma* – references in the scroll hinted at an alliance with a Byzantine scholar.
2. *The Levantine Labyrinth* – tales of a secret sect guarding ancient truths in the heart of the Levant.
3. *The Maghreb Mystery* – rumors of a hidden library deep within the Atlas Mountains.

Her heart raced at the prospect of these new adventures. The recent journey had not only rekindled her love for history but had also ignited a passion for unraveling the intertwined tapestries of civilizations.

Interrupting her reverie, Ismail approached with a curious glint in his eye. "Lost in thought, Laila?" he asked, noticing the list in her journal.

Laila looked up, her eyes shining with enthusiasm. "Just dreaming of the next adventure. The scrolls... they're like a key, not just to Cordoba's past, but perhaps to mysteries beyond."

Ismail, ever the companion in her quests, replied, "Then wherever the winds of history take you, know that you won't be journeying alone."

She smiled, gazing out towards the horizon. The sun was setting, but for Laila, it felt like a new dawn was just beginning.

***

As dusk began to cast its muted palette over Cordoba, the Mezquita stood tall, a beacon of timelessness amidst the ever-changing world. The golden-orange hue of the setting sun illuminated the intricate stonework, making the ancient edifice glow like a jewel.

Laila, Ismail, Farida, and several others gathered in the main plaza of the Mezquita. They were there not for a formal gathering, but simply to bask in the serenity that the place offered.

The hushed whispers of visitors echoed softly, intermingling with the gentle rustle of the trees in the courtyard. The trickling water from the fountains added a rhythmic undertone, like a heartbeat connecting past and present.

Farida, her eyes reflecting the wisdom of ages, said, "This place, it has seen empires rise and fall, heard the prayers of countless souls, and has been the guardian of secrets, both divine and earthly."

Laila, looking up at the vast expanse of arches and columns, replied, "It's more than just bricks and mortar. It's a living testament to our shared journey. And even as we uncover its mysteries, it remains an enigma, reminding us that some things are meant to be felt, not just understood."

Ismail, ever the architect, touched the walls with reverence. "These walls have stories etched into them, not just by the hands that built them, but by every soul that has sought solace here."

The trio sat down, letting the ambiance wash over them. The Mezquita seemed to breathe with them, its walls whispering tales of yesteryears and echoing the hopes of tomorrow.

As the evening deepened, a soft call to prayer resonated, its melodious notes weaving seamlessly with the Mezquita's ambient symphony.

And as the stars began to twinkle overhead, the Mezquita, in all its majestic splendor, stood as a bridge between the heavens and earth - a reminder that mysteries were not just to be solved, but to be revered and cherished.

In that moment, time seemed to stand still, and the Mezquita, with its layers of history and spirituality, promised to remain an eternal guardian of Cordoba's heart and soul.

www.ingramcontent.com/pod-product-compliance
Lightning Source LLC
Chambersburg PA
CBHW032256070726
47590CB00016B/2921